Arthur
the
Tree

World rights reserved. This book or any portion thereof may not be copied or reproduced in any form or manner whatever, except as provided by law, without the written permission of the publisher, except by a reviewer who may quote brief passages in a review.

The author assumes full responsibility for the accuracy of all facts and quotations as cited in this book. The opinions expressed in this book are the author's personal views and interpretations, and do not necessarily reflect those of the publisher.

This book is provided with the understanding that the publisher is not engaged in giving spiritual, legal, medical, or other professional advice. If authoritative advice is needed, the reader should seek the counsel of a competent professional.

Copyright © 2017 Kathie Diamond
Copyright © 2017 TEACH Services, Inc.
ISBN-13: 978-1-4796-0820-1 (Paperback)
ISBN-13: 978-1-4796-0821-8 (ePub)
ISBN-13: 978-1-4796-0822-5 (Mobi)
Library of Congress Control Number: 2017909830

TEACH Services, Inc.
PUBLISHING
www.TEACHServices.com ● (800) 367-1844

Arthur the Tree

Written and Illustrated
By
Kathie Diamond

TEACH Services, Inc.
PUBLISHING
www.TEACHServices.com • (800) 367-1844

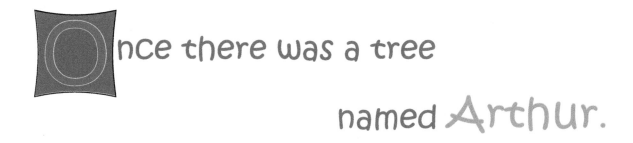

Once there was a tree

named Arthur.

He was a very lonely tree.

No one had played in his branches

for a long time, and

his roots had begun to rot away.

This made Arthur

very sad.

One day,

big, angry storm clouds came.

Rain poured down

and strong winds blew.

Arthur's roots were no longer

strong enough

to hold him up.

While Grandma Birdie

was on a walk,

she saw poor Arthur

and knew he needed help.

Grandma Birdie went home

for her tools.

Grandma Birdie brought

fresh soil for his roots,

clippers for his dead branches,

a rope to help hold him up,

and most important,

lots of love.

With Grandma Birdie's help,

Arthur grew stronger

every day.

His roots went deep into the soil,

and leaves began to

appear on his branches.

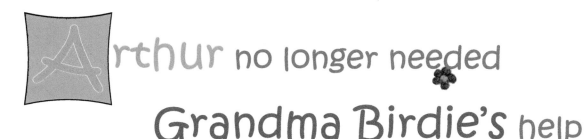

Arthur no longer needed

Grandma Birdie's help

every day.

He had grown into a

strong, healthy tree.

Children once again came to

play in his branches,

and this made Arthur very happy.

God not only wants us to
love and care for
the things of nature
that He has created,
He wants us to
love and care for
each other.

"...be kind to one another,
tenderhearted,
forgiving one another,
even as God in Christ
forgave you."
Ephesians 4:32 (RSV)

TEACH Services, Inc.
P U B L I S H I N G

We invite you to view the complete
selection of titles we publish at:
www.TEACHServices.com

We encourage you to write us
with your thoughts about this,
or any other book we publish at:
info@TEACHServices.com

TEACH Services' titles may be purchased in
bulk quantities for educational, fund-raising,
business, or promotional use.
bulksales@TEACHServices.com

Finally, if you are interested in seeing
your own book in print, please contact us at:
publishing@TEACHServices.com

We are happy to review your manuscript at no charge.

CPSIA information can be obtained
at www.ICGtesting.com
Printed in the USA
LVOW05s1726290617
539734LV00016B/155/P

9 781479 608201